Margret & H. A. Rey's

Curious George
Goes to a Bookstore

Written by Julie M. Bartynski

Illustrated in the style of H. A. Rey *by* Mary O'Keefe Young

HOUGHTON MIFFLIN HARCOURT

Boston   New York

To my husband, Matt, with love —J.M.B.

To my dear siblings Terry, Kathy, Nora, Brendan, Shane, and Danny —M.O'K.Y.

ISBN:978-0-544-32073-4
Printed in China
SCP 10 9 8 7 6 5 4 3 2 1
4500478455

George was a good little monkey and always very curious.

Today George and his friend the man with the yellow hat were going to the grand opening of a bookstore in their neighborhood. George's favorite author was going to be signing her latest Penny the Penguin picture book. He had every Penny book she'd ever written. He couldn't wait to meet her.

But when they arrived at the bookstore, they found a long line that zigzagged between the bookshelves. "We'll purchase the book first and then wait in line to get it signed," said his friend. "There are a lot of kids who also love Penny the Penguin!"

The line inched forward and stopped, inched forward and stopped. George climbed onto his friend's shoulders and tried to take a peek at the author, but he was small and she was hidden by the crowd.

He looked around the bookstore. So many new books! What storie would they hold inside? What funny characters would he meet?

"Be a good little monkey and don't wander off too far," said the man with the yellow hat, letting George down and picking up a bird-watching guide from a nearby shelf. "You wouldn't want to miss getting your book signed."

George was happily flipping through storybooks when he noticed the wonderful smell of banana bread. It made his stomach rumble. George was curious. Could there be food in a bookstore? Food and drink were never allowed in the library. George decided to find out.

As soon as he turned the corner, he discovered glass shelves filled with baked goods instead of books! It was a small café.

Next to the cabinet was a table with a sign advertising free samples.

BANANA
BREAD
TRY ONE

PENNY

George watched people help themselves to little squares of banana bread. He took one too. Yum!

A little girl saw George and tugged on her father's sleeve. "Daddy, look! That monkey likes banana bread too!"

"Yes, I suppose monkeys would enjoy banana bread," he responded, still looking at his book.

While George was reaching for another sample, and then another and another, he saw the little girl and her father leave the café area. Tucked under the girl's arm was George's favorite dinosaur book.

He decided to follow them.

They led him past a display of dinosaur books in the science area of the store. The display was as tall as the man with the yellow hat. It was hard to resist for a little monkey who loves to climb!

George climbed onto the first tier. With so many books to look at, he wasn't sure where to start! He saw his favorite dinosaur book, but he also saw other books. One pictured an apatosaurus eating leaves and another showed pterodactyls soaring above waterfalls.

He climbed from tier to tier until he reached the top. From above he noticed a stack of boxes in the corner of the store. The boxes were shaped like presents, but the bows and wrapping paper were missing.

What could be inside them?

George leaped down
and opened the boxes.

They each contained
a stack of the newest
Penny the Penguin
picture book!

George wondered: Why were the books in boxes? They should be in a big display like the dinosaur books.

George had an idea.

George got to work right away.
He balanced the books one by one,
as if he were building with blocks.

People in line marveled at what he
was doing—except for the man with
the yellow hat, who was engrossed in
his new bird-watching guide.

The tower of books grew and grew and grew, and so did the crowd's amazement.

"What a wonderful display," said a woman.

"Wow, look what that monkey made!" exclaimed a little boy.

"Stop!" shouted a nearby bookseller.
"You shouldn't have opened those boxe

But George
was having too
much fun to
notice.

From the top of his display, George looked down and finally saw the bookseller, the manager, and the man with the yellow hat peering up at him.

"That monkey opened all our boxes for the signing," complained the bookseller.

The manager smiled at George.
"He certainly did, and now we
don't have to. I think his tower of
books is a masterpiece!"

The manager asked George if he
would like to help with the signing.
George was delighted. He would finally
get to meet his favorite author!

George made sure each book was opened to the right page, ready for the author's signature. He thought it was funny that her name was Penny, just like the penguin in her books.

As she finished signing the last book, Penny turned to George and smiled. "Thank you so much for all of your help today. It was great to have the extra hands and feet! But there's one book I still need to sign."

She inscribed the book and handed it to George. Inside was a note saying, "To my new friend George. Keep reading!"

George loved his new book. It was special and one of a kind. He'd had such an adventurous day at the bookstore, he couldn't wait to visit again.

Now You're the Storyteller

The books George found in his bookstore were filled with stories told in both words and pictures. A story has a **beginning, middle,** and **end.** Tell a Curious George story of your own by imagining the beginning, middle, or end that's missing from each of these story snippets below. Share your story by telling it aloud, writing it down, or drawing it!

1) The tour bus driver tells everyone to sit down before she can start driving, but you are sitting next to George and . . . *Create your own beginning!*
What a wild ride! You whizz by the stop at which you were planning to get off—the city zoo—but you don't even notice. There is an elephant following your bus and a troupe of acrobatic monkeys dancing around you. What could be more fun than this perfect end to the day?

2) You invite George and all your friends to your birthday party! You have decorated your house with streamers and balloons. When everyone's there, George decides to take a picture of the whole party from above. But the chandelier he is holding on to starts swinging and George looks like he might go flying into the cake and presents! *What happens next?*
Everyone agrees this is one of the best birthday parties they've ever been to.

3) Your parents have tickets to a baseball game and you get to invite George to come with you!
On the day of the game, both of you wear your baseball jerseys and bring a baseball glove. You sit in the stands and cheer for the home team while eating salty peanuts out of the shells. Suddenly a ball flies over the wall in your direction. *How does this story end?*